Prayer Journal

This book belongs to:

_____

_____

_____

FREE DOWNLOADS

For your FREE Coloring Pages
Visit us at:

http://www.wordofmm.com/

YOUR DOWNLOAD CODE:
PRAYER

date _____

Today's Bible Verse:

_____
_____
_____

How this applies to me

_____
_____
_____
_____

I am grateful for

_____
_____
_____
_____

Notes & requests

_____
_____
_____

date _____

Today's Bible Verse:

How this applies to me

I am grateful for

Notes & requests

date _____

Today's Bible Verse:

How this applies to me

I am grateful for

Notes & requests

date _____

Today's Bible Verse:

How this applies to me

I am grateful for

Notes & requests

date _____

Today's Bible Verse:

How this applies to me

I am grateful for

notes & requests

date_____

Today's Bible Verse:

How this applies to me

I am grateful for

Notes & requests

date _____

Today's Bible Verse:

How this applies to me

I am grateful for

Notes & requests

date _____

Today's Bible Verse:

How this applies to me

I am grateful for

Notes & requests

date_____

Today's Bible Verse:

How this applies to me

I am grateful for

Notes & requests

date _____

Today's Bible Verse:

How this applies to me

I am grateful for

notes & requests

date _____

Today's Bible Verse:

How this applies to me

I am grateful for

Notes & requests

date _____

Today's Bible Verse:

How this applies to me

I am grateful for

Notes & requests

date_____

Today's Bible Verse:

How this applies to me

I am grateful for

Notes & requests

date _____

Today's Bible Verse:

How this applies to me

I am grateful for

Notes & requests

date_____

Today's Bible Verse:

How this applies to me

I am grateful for

Notes & requests

date _____

Today's Bible Verse:

How this applies to me

I am grateful for

notes & requests

date_____

Today's Bible Verse:

How this applies to me

I am grateful for

Notes & requests

date _____

Today's Bible Verse:

How this applies to me

I am grateful for

Notes & requests

date_____

Today's Bible Verse:

How this applies to me

I am grateful for

Notes & requests

date _____

Today's Bible Verse:

How this applies to me

I am grateful for

Notes & requests

date _____

Today's Bible Verse:

How this applies to me

I am grateful for

Notes & requests

date _____

Today's Bible Verse:

How this applies to me

I am grateful for

Notes & requests

date _____

Today's Bible Verse:

How this applies to me

I am grateful for

Notes & requests

date _____

Today's Bible Verse:

How this applies to me

I am grateful for

Notes & requests

date _____

Today's Bible Verse:

How this applies to me

I am grateful for

Notes & requests

date _____

Today's Bible Verse:

How this applies to me

I am grateful for

Notes & requests

date_____

Today's Bible Verse:

How this applies to me

I am grateful for

Notes & requests

date _____

Today's Bible Verse:

How this applies to me

I am grateful for

Notes & requests

date_____

Today's Bible Verse:

How this applies to me

I am grateful for

notes & requests

date _____

Today's Bible Verse:

How this applies to me

I am grateful for

Notes & requests

date _____

Today's Bible Verse:

How this applies to me

I am grateful for

Notes & requests

date _____

Today's Bible Verse:

How this applies to me

I am grateful for

notes & requests

date_____

Today's Bible Verse:

_____
_____
_____

How this applies to me

_____
_____
_____
_____

I am grateful for

_____
_____
_____
_____

Notes & requests

_____
_____
_____
_____

date _____

Today's Bible Verse:

How this applies to me

I am grateful for

notes & requests

date _____

Today's Bible Verse:

How this applies to me

I am grateful for

Notes & requests

date _____

Today's Bible Verse:

How this applies to me

I am grateful for

Notes & requests

date_____

Today's Bible Verse:

How this applies to me

I am grateful for

Notes & requests

date _____

Today's Bible Verse:

How this applies to me

I am grateful for

Notes & requests

date_____

Today's Bible Verse:

How this applies to me

I am grateful for

Notes & requests

date _____

Today's Bible Verse:

How this applies to me

I am grateful for

Notes & requests

date_____

Today's Bible Verse:

How this applies to me

I am grateful for

Notes & requests

date _____

Today's Bible Verse:

How this applies to me

I am grateful for

Notes & requests

date _____

Today's Bible Verse:

How this applies to me

I am grateful for

Notes & requests

date _____

Today's Bible Verse:

How this applies to me

I am grateful for

notes & requests

date _____

Today's Bible Verse:

How this applies to me

I am grateful for

Notes & requests

date _____

Today's Bible Verse:

How this applies to me

I am grateful for

notes & requests

date _____

Today's Bible Verse:

How this applies to me

I am grateful for

Notes & requests

date _____

Today's Bible Verse:

How this applies to me

I am grateful for

Notes & requests

date_____

Today's Bible Verse:

How this applies to me

I am grateful for

Notes & requests

date _____

Today's Bible Verse:

How this applies to me

I am grateful for

Notes & requests

date_____

Today's Bible Verse:

How this applies to me

I am grateful for

Notes & requests

Today's Bible Verse:

How this applies to me

I am grateful for

Notes & requests

date _____

Today's Bible Verse:

_____
_____
_____

How this applies to me

_____
_____
_____
_____

I am grateful for

_____
_____
_____
_____

notes & requests

_____
_____
_____
_____

date _____

Today's Bible Verse:

How this applies to me

I am grateful for

Notes & requests

date_____

Today's Bible Verse:

_____
_____
_____

How this applies to me

_____
_____
_____
_____

I am grateful for

_____
_____
_____
_____

Notes & requests

_____
_____
_____
_____

date _____

Today's Bible Verse:

How this applies to me

I am grateful for

Notes & requests

date_____

Today's Bible Verse:

How this applies to me

I am grateful for

Notes & requests

date _____

Today's Bible Verse:

How this applies to me

I am grateful for

Notes & requests

date _____

Today's Bible Verse:

How this applies to me

I am grateful for

notes & requests

date _____

Today's Bible Verse:

How this applies to me

I am grateful for

Notes & requests

date_____

Today's Bible Verse:

_____
_____
_____

How this applies to me

_____
_____
_____
_____

I am grateful for

_____
_____
_____
_____

notes & requests

_____
_____
_____
_____

Today's Bible Verse:

How this applies to me

I am grateful for

notes & requests

date _____

Today's Bible Verse:

How this applies to me

I am grateful for

Notes & requests

date _____

Today's Bible Verse:

How this applies to me

I am grateful for

Notes & requests

date _____

Today's Bible Verse:

How this applies to me

I am grateful for

Notes & requests

date_____

Today's Bible Verse:

How this applies to me

I am grateful for

Notes & requests

date_____

Today's Bible Verse:

How this applies to me

I am grateful for

notes & requests

date_____

Today's Bible Verse:

How this applies to me

I am grateful for

Notes & requests

date_____

Today's Bible Verse:

_____
_____
_____

How this applies to me

_____
_____
_____
_____

I am grateful for

_____
_____
_____
_____

Notes & requests

_____
_____
_____
_____

date _____

Today's Bible Verse:

How this applies to me

I am grateful for

Notes & requests

date _____

Today's Bible Verse:

How this applies to me

I am grateful for

Notes & requests

date _____

Today's Bible Verse:

How this applies to me

I am grateful for

notes & requests

date_____

Today's Bible Verse:

How this applies to me

I am grateful for

Notes & requests

date _____

Today's Bible Verse:

How this applies to me

I am grateful for

Notes & requests

date_____

Today's Bible Verse:

How this applies to me

I am grateful for

notes & requests

date _____

Today's Bible Verse:

How this applies to me

I am grateful for

Notes & requests

date_____

Today's Bible Verse:

How this applies to me

I am grateful for

Notes & requests

date _____

Today's Bible Verse:

How this applies to me

I am grateful for

notes & requests

date_____

Today's Bible Verse:

How this applies to me

I am grateful for

Notes & requests

date _____

Today's Bible Verse:

How this applies to me

I am grateful for

Notes & requests

date_____

Today's Bible Verse:

How this applies to me

I am grateful for

Notes & requests

date _____

Today's Bible Verse:

How this applies to me

I am grateful for

Notes & requests

date _____

Today's Bible Verse:

How this applies to me

I am grateful for

Notes & requests

date _____

Today's Bible Verse:

How this applies to me

I am grateful for

notes & requests

date_____

Today's Bible Verse:

How this applies to me

I am grateful for

Notes & requests

date _____

Today's Bible Verse:

_____
_____
_____

How this applies to me

_____
_____
_____
_____

I am grateful for

_____
_____
_____
_____

Notes & requests

_____
_____
_____
_____

date _____

Today's Bible Verse:

_____
_____
_____

How this applies to me

_____
_____
_____

I am grateful for

_____
_____
_____

Notes & requests

_____
_____
_____

Today's Bible Verse:

How this applies to me

I am grateful for

Notes & requests

date_____

Today's Bible Verse:

How this applies to me

I am grateful for

notes & requests

date _____

Today's Bible Verse:

How this applies to me

I am grateful for

Notes & requests

date _____

Today's Bible Verse:

How this applies to me

I am grateful for

notes & requests

date _____

Today's Bible Verse:

How this applies to me

I am grateful for

Notes & requests

date _____

Today's Bible Verse:

How this applies to me

I am grateful for

Notes & requests

date_____

Today's Bible Verse:

How this applies to me

I am grateful for

notes & requests

date_____

Today's Bible Verse:

How this applies to me

I am grateful for

Notes & requests

date _____

Today's Bible Verse:

How this applies to me

I am grateful for

Notes & requests

date_____

Today's Bible Verse:

How this applies to me

I am grateful for

Notes & requests

date _____

Today's Bible Verse:

How this applies to me

I am grateful for

Notes & requests

date _____

Today's Bible Verse:

How this applies to me

I am grateful for

notes & requests

date _____

Today's Bible Verse:

How this applies to me

I am grateful for

notes & requests

date_____

Today's Bible Verse:

_____
_____
_____

How this applies to me

_____
_____
_____
_____

I am grateful for

_____
_____
_____
_____

Notes & requests

_____
_____
_____
_____

date _____

Today's Bible Verse:

How this applies to me

I am grateful for

Notes & requests

date_____

Today's Bible Verse:

_____
_____
_____

How this applies to me

_____
_____
_____
_____

I am grateful for

_____
_____
_____
_____

Notes & requests

_____
_____
_____
_____

date_____

Today's Bible Verse:

How this applies to me

I am grateful for

Notes & requests